To all the grandmothers out there making magic.

To two grandmothers in particular.

You know who you are . . .

Serena Holly

To my two wonderful Grandmas

who continue to inspire me.

Selom Sunu

CHAPTER ONE

'Magic!' Granny Jinks exclaimed, clapping her hands as Jada carefully placed the final brown sugar cube at the top of the already-swaying pyramid.

Jada held her breath as she watched her Ancient Egypt history homework wobble from side to side. She let it out again when it stayed upright.

'Say cheese! Or, wait, say, "pyramids"!'

Granny grabbed her phone and took a photo of Jada with her handiwork. 'Now, remind me, how do I upload this to your school worky-space?'

Jada giggled and showed her grandmother how to get to the right folder again. 'I'm really not sure my teacher is going to count this as homework.'

'Of course, she will,' Granny insisted. 'It's history and engineering all in one! What's not to like?'

Jada smiled. She loved coming to Granny Jinks's house after school. Granny made everything fun – even homework. She liked it best when they had the music blasting, and they danced together around the mismatched furniture in the front room. Granny had painted all of her wooden chairs in rainbow colours a few months ago, just for fun. Jada had helped – she'd painted the one she was sitting on orange and purple.

Jada's dad always said that Granny Jinks was a bit **EXTRA**, but Jada loved her grandmother just the way she was. Jada and her dad lived in a neat and tidy house, with a neat and tidy driveway edged with neat and tidy flowerbeds. The small garden out the back had an evenly clipped, neat and tidy lawn that Dad mowed for exactly twenty-three minutes every Saturday morning.

Messy play? Arts and crafts? Hah! No way! *Dad won't even let me touch a paintbrush back at our*

4

house, Jada thought. Her dad would worry that the paint was toxic, or that it might spill all over his carefully mopped floors. *I'm eight years old now – as if I'd spill paint!* Jada sighed to herself.

With a mum as fun as Granny Jinks, sometimes Jada wondered how Dad had turned out the way he had. He wore black or grey suits to work every day, with the same grey socks, and the same shiny black shoes.

Jada was pretty sure Granny didn't own a *single* item of grey clothing. Right now, her grandmother was wearing a purple cardigan over a green-and-white striped cotton dress. Her short, thick afro hair was laced with silver strands, and she often stuck her glasses or spare pens into

5

it for safekeeping (then forgot they were there!).

'Hmmm,' Granny Jinks said. 'You know what I think would help even *more* with your Ancient Egypt homework, my gem?' She reached out and plucked one of the sugar cubes from the middle of the pyramid, dropping it into her teacup as she spoke. Jada stared, amazed that the tower didn't topple. Granny winked, pleased with her trick.

Jada grinned. 'No, what?'

Granny Jinks leaned in. 'We need to *really* get into the Ancient Egyptians' heads. To think about all their magic and mystery. So – we need costumes! I probably have a cape somewhere in my closet that is absolutely fit for a pharaoh! Ooh, and maybe a staff, too . . . Why don't you

go have a rummage and see what
you can find?'

Smiling, Jada darted up the stairs
to Granny's bedroom. On the way,
she stopped briefly to wink and
blow a kiss to the framed poster of
Grandpa Jinks in the hall.

Once she reached the top, she flung open the
door to Granny's bedroom. The room was filled
with oversized flowering plants, so it smelled
amazing, as usual.

Luna, Granny's cat, was lying on top of the
multicoloured bedspread with all four of her
paws in the air, and her little pink
tongue lolling out of one side of her

mouth. Jada went over to tickle the fuzzy black fur on the cat's tummy, and Luna let out a sleepy purr-bark. Sometimes she acted and sounded more like a dog than a cat!

Of all the fantastic places in Granny Jinks's house, her special closet was the *most* magical. It was more a tiny room than a cupboard really, bursting with costume pieces, funny hats, feather boas, sparkling ballgowns and cowboy boots.

Granny Jinks used to work at the Dalton Green Theatre and had collected a *lot* of things over the years. She always said she'd collected her husband in the theatre too.

Jada loved that story. She knew all about Grandpa Jinks, and how they'd fallen in love while Granny was the theatre's stage manager, overseeing all the costumes and sets. Grandpa Jinks was a magician. He toured all over the country with his show. His most famous trick was the **INGENIOUS JINKS'S DISAPPEARING ACT**. Even Granny didn't know how he pulled it off!

Jada opened the closet door and jumped up to tug on the pull-cord inside to switch on the light. Her elbow knocked into a wooden box on the shelf. It was overflowing, just like everything else in Granny Jinks's closet, and it tumbled down, spilling its contents out onto the floor and onto Jada!

'Whoops!' she exclaimed, narrowly dodging

a feathery carnival headdress as it fell to the ground. Never mind, she'd tidy it up later.

On the floor, under a tangle of colourful scarves, Jada found a gold headdress. *Perfect for a pharaoh*, she thought, pulling it on over her braided hair. Digging further, she found some chunky wooden bracelets and a set of fairy wings, but couldn't find the cape Granny was talking about.

Then she noticed a magician's wand. *Hmm . . . Did Ancient Egyptians use magic wands?* She leaned down to pick it up and looked at it carefully. What was it Granny always said? 'Find the magic in any situation' . . . ? Jada was about to walk away, back downstairs to Granny, but froze

as she noticed something else that had fallen out
of the box.

'**Eww!**' she shrieked.

Lying amid the mess on the closet floor was . . .

'A THUMB?!'

CHAPTER TWO

'Yuck, yuck, *yuck*!' Jada jumped up and covered her eyes.

Then she shook her head.

Get a grip, Jada Jinks, she told herself. *It's not going to be real, is it?*

Jada peeked between her fingers and cautiously poked the thumb with her foot to check it out more thoroughly. It was hard to tell if it was real or not through her sock. Sucking in a breath, Jada bent down and picked it up. It felt like rubber. 'Fake,' she said, relieved. 'Phew!' *But why would Granny have a fake thumb in her cupboard?* she wondered, frowning.

She peered more closely at the box the thumb had fallen out of. It was large, red and glittery. On each side it had a curly 'I' and 'J' with stars bursting out from around the letters. Jada picked up the lid. In swirling silver writing, it said:

The Ingenious Jinks's Box of Tricks!

Could this be . . . Grandpa Jinks's magic box?

Jada knew that her grandfather had been an incredible magician and people came from far and wide to see him. Years ago, you would only have to hear the name 'Jinks' and people's eyes would light up with excitement.

But Dad didn't really like to talk about Grandpa Jinks. He died a long time ago, when Jada's dad was little. Granny told her Grandpa's tour bus had had an accident one night when he was away doing his magic shows. Since then, Dad had always been wary of magic, and even the theatre. For him, magic and tricks were dangerous. After all, it was magic that took his dad away for ever.

Dad was a bit better at talking about Jada's mum, even though she wasn't around at the moment either. Jada knew her mum loved her (in her own special kind of way) but Mum wasn't very good at staying in one place. She was a singer and needed to go where the gigs were. In her letters, Mum always said it was better for everyone that she wasn't around – she'd just mess things up.

Jada knew that Dad understood how much it hurt to miss a parent. Especially when you were still a kid. He was always there if Jada was getting sad about her mum, and he always knew exactly what to do. Like if she was looking at old photos and wanted to cry, he'd give her a hug and then cheer her up by cooking her favourite dish – lasagne à la Dad, with extra cinnamon and black pepper. She'd help to make the white sauce and he'd clean up behind her. They made a good team, Dad and Jada.

Jada sniffed and wiped her nose on her sleeve. Then she quickly gathered up the *The Ingenious Jinks's Box of Tricks!* – fake thumb included – and ran downstairs.

'Granny!' she called, plonking the box on the cluttered dining table. 'Look what I've found!'

Granny Jinks looked surprised, then grinned broadly. 'A-ha! Yes, that box has some of your grandpa's old magic gear in it.' She reached in and pulled out a spotted silk handkerchief and held it to her cheek. 'He used to wear this in the top pocket of his costume. He was so dapper. And he used it for disappearing tricks too – look.'

Granny plucked another sugar lump from the pyramid and held it in her left palm. Then she draped the silk hankie over it, counted to three and – *whoosh!* When she swept the handkerchief away with a flourish, the sugar lump was gone!

Jada clapped extra hard when Granny magically found the sugar lump behind her ear.

Granny gave a little bow in her seat. 'Oh, I miss him, Jada Gem. I miss the theatre, too.'

'That must be why you made this house so dramatic!' Jada's grin was cheeky.

Granny laughed. 'You're not wrong, Jada Gem!

18

Now, what are you hiding in that hand of yours?'

Jada unfurled her fingers and showed Granny the fake thumb. 'Do you recognise this?'

'Of course I do!' Granny Jinks picked it up and held it beside her own thumb. 'Your grandpa was so proud of this. "A proper work of art," he'd say. You see that?' she said, comparing her warm brown skin to the prop. 'Nearly a perfect match! Your grandpa had it made specially because he couldn't find any fake thumbs in the right shade for him back in the day . . .' She frowned for a moment, then peered harder at it, pulling her glasses out of her hair and putting them on to get a closer look. 'I tell you, he could do all sorts of trickery with this little guy. Look – it's hollow inside and I think it has some kind of suction pad. Cedric could even make things float with it!'

'Wow!' Jada said, leaning in to get a better look.

Granny Jinks played around with the thumb a bit, then shook her head. 'I'm afraid I don't quite remember how to use it. A magician NEVER reveals their tricks, but I did try to work this one

out from watching your grandpa perform all those years ago . . .' She popped the thumb onto the table and reached into the box again. 'Now, I might not know how to work the magic thumb, but your granny knows plenty of card tricks. Prepare to be amazed!' Granny Jinks pulled out a small red packet, shook out the cards and began to shuffle them. 'These ones are special, with extra slipperiness to make the tricks easier. Pick a card, any card. Don't tell me what it is,' she said, fanning them out so only Jada could see the numbers.

Jada pointed to the eight of hearts. Eight was her favourite number and she loved to doodle hearts on her notebooks. She watched in awe as her grandmother shuffled the cards super-fast, concertinaed them, then shuffled them again. Granny Jinks fanned the cards out once more between her hands, and then the eight of hearts seemed to magically float out above the others in the pack.

Jada clapped excitedly. 'That's amazing! That's my card, Granny! How did you do that?'

Granny Jinks winked her special wink she did just for Jada. They called it the **'Jinks wink'**. 'Magic, my girl! When I was a young woman, it used to cross my mind every once in a while that I'd be a rather magnificent magician myself. We used to speak about it, me and Grandpa. He thought I had a special knack.' She sighed. 'Just a bit of silly talk.'

Jada frowned. 'Why's it silly? I think you'd be an amazing magician, Granny! Why don't you just start learning more magic now?'

Granny Jinks made a funny bubbling noise that seemed to start deep down in her belly. Then

it got louder and louder, until she was roaring
with . . . laughter?

'What's so funny?' Jada asked.

'Learn to be a magician? Me? Now?' Granny
Jinks said in between chuckles. 'At my big, big
age?' She smacked her palm against the table in
her amusement. The pyramid stayed up but the
thumb rolled off the dining table and onto the
floor. Luna trotted into the room at the sound
of Granny's laughter, miaow-barking as though
she was laughing too, and then Jada heard an all-
too-familiar noise.

'Wait, is that Dad's car door shutting?' Jada
asked, startled. 'Is he here?' She stared at the box
and the magic props spread all over the table.

25

Dad hates magic, Jada thought. She pulled the gold headdress off her head, her gaze darting from the box to the hankie to the pyramid. *Dad mustn't see this!* 'Quick, Granny, we need to tidy all this away now!'

CHAPTER THREE

'Mum? Jada?' Dad's voice echoed in the hallway as he opened the front door.

Jada stashed Grandpa Jinks's box under the dining table. Quickly, Granny cleared away the props and then the pyramid as well so there would be no talk of magical Egyptians. She plonked the last of the remaining sugar cubes into her teacup and looked up as Jonny Jinks walked into the living room.

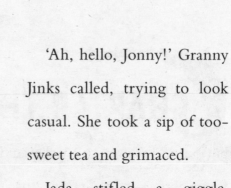

'Ah, hello, Jonny!' Granny Jinks called, trying to look casual. She took a sip of too-sweet tea and grimaced.

Jada stifled a giggle. 'Hiya, Dad,' she said, giving him a hug. Then she spied Grandpa Jinks's spotted silk handkerchief on the table! Widening her eyes at Granny, she quickly shoved it into her pocket without her dad noticing. *Phew.*

'Hey! Sorry I'm late – parents' evening ran over a bit.' Jonny Jinks put his briefcase down.

Now it was Jada's turn to grimace. *Uh-oh!* She'd forgotten *all* about parents' evening.

Loosening his tie a bit, Jada's dad undid the button on his grey suit jacket and folded his tall frame into one of Granny Jinks's bright purple armchairs. He brushed away the backrest's long tassels that tried to tickle his face. Jada sat on a chair next to him.

'So, what did the teachers say about our fabulous Jada?' Granny asked, standing up.

'Lots of good things, really good things, but Miss Benson also told me that you've been having some trouble with your maths, Jada.' He reached a hand out to rub his daughter's shoulder. 'You're refusing to answer when she asks you a question?'

Jada looked down and scuffed a toe along the fluffy yellow rug on the living-room floor, remembering her teacher and all her classmates waiting expectantly for her to say something. It wasn't that she didn't know the answers. Maths always made sense to her on the page. It was just when she had to explain the numbers out loud in front of everyone that she went all wobbly. She never much liked talking to the whole class, but maths made her extra shy for some reason. Even just thinking about it made her face all hot.

'Well?' Dad questioned. 'Come on, sweetheart, you know how important maths is! It got me—'

'Where you are today, I know, I know,' Jada mumbled. Dad was very fond of pointing out

that he'd known all his times tables at her age. Apparently, he'd also wanted to be an accountant since he was a baby.

Dad's neat moustache curved as he smiled sympathetically at her. 'Well, not to worry, Jada Gem! We're going to sort it all out. We Jinkses are problem solvers – remember? Miss Benson told me that there's some after-school tuition on offer at the community centre. So guess what?'

Jada raised her eyebrows. She had a feeling she wasn't going to like the answer . . .

'I went there and signed you up for some extra maths classes!'

'Dad!' Jada looked at him pleadingly. 'I don't need extra maths—'

'But if you can't answer the questions, maybe you do need some help?' Dad interrupted, confused.

Jada was feeling a bit flustered now, just like in maths classes! She glanced over at Granny Jinks, who had folded her arms and was tapping her foot. *Her battle stance*, Jada thought.

'Now, Jonny,' Granny said. 'Are you sure she needs to do all of that?'

Dad nodded. 'It'll be really good for Jada — and it'll take a bit of pressure off you, too, Mum.' He glanced around the living room and peered through into the kitchen. 'I mean, taking care of Jada every day after school and keeping this place neat and tidy must be a lot for you . . .'

Granny Jinks put her hands on her hips. 'Facety!' she said.

'I wasn't being rude, Mum. I just wonder if you need to slow down.' Dad frowned as he spotted something across the room. He stood up and straightened a picture of a leopard hanging above the mantelpiece.

Jada and her granny exchanged a *look*.

'Slow down? Me?!' Granny scowled. 'What a cheek. And about this mathematics thing. I'd miss Jada if I didn't see her every day after school.'

'Oh, Granny!' Jada jumped up and gave Granny a big hug.

'I thought you'd say that,' Dad said, picking up his briefcase and popping it open. 'Which is why I picked up these leaflets at the community centre. They have lots of craft classes there, too. Relaxing things, like crochet. Maybe you and Jada could go together after school? You know, she can do her maths and you can do . . . more things that other grandparents do?'

Granny Jinks raised an eyebrow so high Jada thought it might take off. '*I*,' she declared, 'am not like other grandparents!'

'Don't I know it,' Jada's dad said under his breath.

'Me? I have plenty of energy!' Granny Jinks started to do star-jumps in the middle of the living-room floor.

Jada joined in, giggling. 'Yeah, Dad, Granny

Jinks has loooads of energy,' she said between jumps. 'And I love coming here. It's the most fun ever!'

'All right, all right,' Dad said, smiling a bit. 'But I want you both to give the classes at the community centre a go. For me? They start the day after tomorrow.'

Jada and Granny both came to a stop, panting. Inwardly, Jada added a groan. She knew Dad wouldn't change his mind about the extra maths lessons. But she'd been looking forward to going through the box of tricks again. Plus she needed to put her plan in action, the Get Granny to Become a Magician Plan. These maths classes would just be a distraction.

Dad closed his briefcase, picked it up and moved towards the dining table to grab Jada's school bag. 'Right, Jada Gem, go get your coat. We should be—' He broke off as Luna darted between his legs. She was batting something eagerly between her paws and letting out another strange bark-miaow! Dad rolled his eyes. 'This cat gets more random every time I come here, Mum! Are you sure she's all right?'

Luna wiggled her fuzzy black behind in the air, her eyes trained eagerly on her 'prey'.

Jada glanced down, and her eyes widened as she saw what Luna was playing with – it was Grandpa Jinks's magic thumb, and it was only a few centimetres away from Jada's dad's very shiny leather shoes! If he saw it, he'd know that she and Granny had been messing about with the box of tricks.

Jonny Jinks squinted at the strange object lying on the floor. 'What is that . . . ?' he began, bending down to get a closer look, but Jada was quicker than him.

'I'll check for you!' Jada dived towards Luna.

'Jada! What are you doing?' Dad asked as she scrabbled about on the floor.

Jada quickly grabbed the thumb, while Luna growled, then jumped up.

'She's just saying goodbye to my sweet little kitty, aren't you, Jada Gem?' Granny Jinks said, scooping the cat up. Luna protested a little more, then began purring loudly and nuzzled close.

Jada gave her dad her best nothing-to-see-here grin. 'Yep! That's it!' She slipped the thumb into the pocket of her shorts, and took his hand, leading him out of the door. 'Bye-bye, Granny!'

Bemused, Dad blew Granny Jinks a goodbye kiss, before following Jada out of the door.

Jada turned to wave at Granny, and gave her another quick wink while Dad wasn't looking.

Granny gave a **Jinks wink** back, but Jada noticed she was wearing a little frown as they walked away. Suddenly Jada felt like a small stone was sitting in her stomach. After-school maths would be nowhere near as fun as going to Granny's house.

CHAPTER FOUR

The next morning, Jada watched as Benji's dad chatted happily to Tolu's mum at the school gates.

Jada's dad had just pulled away in his car. He never had time to hang about and chat with the other parents. He always had to rush off to work, and have meetings about things like financial planning and budgets and other boring grown-up office stuff.

That's why Jada was so glad to have Granny Jinks to look after her when school finished each day. Though Jada had to admit that sometimes her granny stood out a bit *too* much in her quirky, colourful clothes, with Luna perched in her special cat bag!

Jada loved spending time with her granny and her dad, but sometimes – just sometimes – she wished she fitted in a bit more with the other kids at her school. And, most of all, she wished that her mum lived close enough to collect her.

As she walked into the playground, Jada suddenly noticed a girl she hadn't seen before. She had long brown hair, and looked about Jada's

age. She was being dropped off by a teenager in a cool, swishy dress and trainers.

'Have a good first day, Matilda,' the teenager said, giving the younger girl a big hug. 'See you later!'

'Bye, sis!' Matilda called in reply, giving a big wave. Despite Matilda's loud, enthusiastic goodbye, once her sister had rounded the corner away from the school, Jada noticed that the girl's smile disappeared. She watched as Matilda glanced around the playground, shuffling her feet, then fiddling with her backpack zip.

She must be new, Jada thought to herself.

Just then, Jada saw a football flying across the playground – straight towards the new girl!

'Matilda! Watch out!' she yelled.

The girl looked up and, with no fuss at all, jumped for the ball and headed it away. But as she did so, she dropped her backpack and everything spilled out onto the ground.

'Nice header, new girl!' Jayden called from the other end of the playground as he took the ball onto the inside of his foot and then dribbled it past Benji and Mo.

Matilda flicked her long wavy hair out of her eyes, and bent down to pick up her things.

Before she could even think about being shy, Jada dashed over to help her. On the ground were her pencil case, lunchbox and some pocket tissues. Next to those things was a small red packet that looked very familiar. It was a box of the exact same brand of playing cards she'd found in *Grandpa Jinks's Box of Tricks* – the extra slippery ones that magicians used for better shuffling!

'Oh, thanks a lot,' Matilda said, as Jada reached down to help pick up her bits and pieces.

'No worries.' Jada smiled, handing the cards back. 'These are for magic, right? My granny has the exact same pack at home. My grandpa was a magician!'

The new girl grinned and Jada noticed she had a spray of freckles across her pale cheeks.

'A real magician?' Matilda asked. 'Like on stage and everything?'

'Yes, that's right. He was called the Ingenious Jinks,' Jada said. She couldn't understand why she was talking so much. She never did that! Not at school, anyway.

'*Nice!*' said Matilda, clearly impressed.

'Do you know any tricks?' Jada asked.

Matilda responded with a wink that reminded Jada of Granny. 'Might do!' Matilda stuck out her hand, and Jada smiled as she shook it. 'Thanks for the heads-up about the ball, by the way. I go by Tilda, actually.'

'Ah, okay. I'm Jada,' she said. 'Is it your first day?'

Tilda nodded. 'Yeah, my family and I move around quite a lot.'

47

'It must be nice to see lots of new places.'

'It is, but it can be hard to start in a new place sometimes,' Matilda said. Her expression was proud and sort of sad at the same time.

Jada nodded. 'I guess it can be tricky making friends? I've been at this school for ever and I still feel a bit shy sometimes.' She looked around the playground. 'I've never met anyone else who's into magic before!'

Tilda's face brightened. 'Magic helps with getting to know people. I've only just started learning tricks, but I'm really into it. Especially stuff with cards. My mum always tells me I'm a bit of a fidget, and this keeps my hands busy.' She flicked the pack of cards from one hand to the other in an impressive concertina.

'Wow!' Jada said in awe.

'I've been practising.' Tilda smiled as she shuffled the cards. 'I'm going to audition for the *Dalton Green Magic Society* tomorrow. It's after school at the community centre.'

Jada's ears pricked up. 'Really? I have to go there tomorrow for some sort of extra maths lessons.' Her stomach did a little flip at the thought of having to speak in front of a whole new maths class.

Tilda pulled a face. 'Ugh, that sounds like no fun.'

'Thing is,' Jada continued, a plan hatching in her mind, 'my Granny Jinks loves magic, too. It would be so cool if she could come and audition for the Magic Society!'

'Why doesn't she?' Tilda asked, her green eyes lighting up. 'Then you could come too. It'd be great to see a friendly face in the audience!'

Jada bit her lip. 'But I have the maths lesson, and Granny Jinks is meant to be in some crochet class. I don't know how we'd get out of it. My dad would be really annoyed if he heard I missed my maths lesson . . .'

Tilda raised an eyebrow. 'Well, the auditions will go on for a while. You could try to breeze through the maths questions and get out early!'

'Maybe . . .' Jada said. The trouble was, even if she aced the lesson, Jada knew her dad wouldn't be happy about her having anything to do with magic.

'Well, no problem if you can't,' Tilda said, standing a little straighter. Even though Jada had only just met her, she could tell that Tilda was a little disappointed. Maybe she wasn't as confident as she was trying to seem.

Suddenly, something Granny Jinks always said popped into Jada's mind – 'Diamonds are formed under pressure – like you, Jada Gem!'

Tilda was a diamond, Jada was sure.

'We'll make it happen!' Jada said, and stuck out her elbow just as the bell went. Grinning, Tilda looped her arm through Jada's, and together they ran into school.

CHAPTER FIVE

Jada peered out at the grey clouds gathering in the sky as she and her classmates spilled out into the playground after the final school bell. The gloomy sky fitted Jada's mood. The time had finally arrived. She was *not* looking forward to going to maths tutoring at the community centre. Especially since she still hadn't come up with a *proper* plan to get her granny to the Magic

Society auditions that were also happening that evening. She hadn't even told Granny about them. What was the point if they couldn't go?

Jada waved as she spotted Granny Jinks chatting to Benji's mum at the school gates. It was hard to miss her, in her bright yellow raincoat and apple-green swishing skirt. And, of course, Luna was miaow-barking from her special cat bag over Granny's shoulder.

'How was school, Jada Gem?' Granny asked as she approached. 'And your new friend Tilda?' Jada perked up for a minute to tell her about the three-cups-and-a-ball trick she'd been helping Tilda practise at break time.

'Ahh, a classic,' Granny Jinks said with a smile.

'We could have a go at doing that at home . . .'
she trailed off. 'But I suppose we'd better be
getting ourselves over to the community centre.
You've got a class to go to, eh? And I'll be getting
familiar with balls of wool . . .'

Granny Jinks was trying to sound enthusiastic, but Jada could tell she was looking forward to her crochet class about as much as Jada was to her extra maths lessons.

They waved goodbye to Benji and his mum and set off. Jada looked out for Tilda as they walked, but she couldn't see her. Tilda must have raced ahead to get to the Magic Society auditions on time. Jada wished she'd been able to go with her.

Soon, they came to a stop outside a large red-brick building. It had shiny silver letters on the front:

DALTON GREEN
COMMUNITY CENTRE
A PLACE FOR ALL

'Here we are, then,' Granny Jinks said. There was definitely no excitement in her voice. Then she turned to Jada, a small smile curving her lips, which were painted in her favourite shade of red lipstick. 'Well, Jada Gem, I know we'd both rather be having some fun back at the house, but since we're here, we might as well make the most of it. We'll do it for your Dad, what d'you say?' Granny Jinks held out one of her strong, warm, softly wrinkled hands.

Jada took it, drew herself up taller and nodded. She shook Granny Jinks's hand, then gave her a high-five – their own secret handshake – and returned her smile. 'Okay, Granny. You're right. Let's go.'

They checked the noticeboard just inside the entrance to the community centre. There were posters for all kinds of activities, including pottery-making, finger-painting and, down at the bottom, one for the Magic Society auditions.

Jada noticed that Granny's eyes rested on the poster for just a second. Jada opened her mouth to say something but stopped herself. *There's no point*, she thought. *Granny won't go by herself and she will never agree to me going to the auditions over the maths lesson.* They both knew how important it was to Dad.

Jada found the notice for her maths tutor group, which said it was in the library at the end of the corridor. Crochet Club was right next door. They headed down the hallway and reached Crochet Club first. Jada poked her head round the door and saw a handful of older people in cardigans and thick-knit jumpers gathering round a table that had a small plate of very boring

biscuits on it. *Not the only thing that looks boring here*, Jada thought.

Granny frowned. 'Can I come to maths with you?' she asked hopefully, and they both giggled. 'Okay, sweetheart, the library is just next door. Do you want me to take you in?'

Jada shook her head. 'No, thanks, Granny. I'll be fine.' She swallowed. *If Granny Jinks can do this, so can I.*

They waved goodbye to each other, and Jada pushed open the library door. She felt four sets of eyes turn towards her as the other kids who were there for tutoring looked up. She thought she recognised two of them from her school — a girl with messy pigtails, and a boy with glasses which he kept pushing up his nose. There were also two girls huddled together chatting at one desk, whose sleek black bob haircuts and big dark eyes were almost identical to one another. Jada realised they must be twins.

'Ah, you must be Jada Jinks!' said a soft, musical-sounding voice. Jada looked towards the front of the room and saw a tall lady with short dark wavy hair and a kind face. 'I'm Miss Mendel. Come in, come in, grab a seat and join our merry mathematical team! We're just about to start.'

Jada walked over to a free desk and sat down, exchanging a shy smile with the pigtail girl.

'So, Jada, this is Rosalia,' Miss Mendel said, smiling at them both. 'That's Femi,' she said, nodding towards the boy with glasses. 'And here we have the Wang twins, Lisa and Linda.'

Lisa and Linda waved in a friendly way then went straight back to chatting.

Miss Mendel picked up some sheets of paper from the table in front of her, then came over and popped one down on each of their desks. She gently told the twins to shush, and Jada noticed that their tutor had a lovely sweet perfume that wafted around her, matching her friendly smile.

Oh no! Jada thought as she studied the paper Miss Mendel had placed in front of her. This tutoring session was going to be even worse than she'd thought. The sums and maths problems on the sheet seemed far too easy and boring. Jada never had trouble doing maths on the page – the numbers behaved for her there. It was speaking up and answering questions out loud that she found hard. Just thinking about having to do that now, in front of people who were practically strangers, made Jada's tummy jumble like it was full of jumping beans.

Miss Mendel clapped her hands together. 'Okay, wonderful. What I thought we could do today is work through these sums on the pages I've handed out to you. Then I can see how you're all getting on with your maths now, and where you might need help.'

Jada picked up her pencil and quickly began working through the maths problems on the page. As she had expected, none of the questions were difficult. *I wonder how Granny Jinks is doing in Crochet Club*, Jada thought. If only she had worked out a way to get Granny over to the

Magic Society auditions instead of that dull-looking craft class! *Maybe if I finish with the maths worksheet early, I'll be able to get out of the class and—*

'Gosh, you're racing through these, Jada!'

Jada jumped at Miss Mendel's voice and looked up to see the maths tutor smiling warmly down at her.

'Let's take a look, shall we?' Miss Mendel said, crouching down to see Jada's work. 'Good stuff! You're doing really well here, Jada,' the tutor told her encouragingly. 'It's so helpful to get an idea of what you already know. Since you've almost finished with these, let me dig out a few more exercises for you to try that might challenge you a bit more.'

Miss Mendel stood back up. Jada glanced over at the door longingly and noticed another Magic Society poster stuck on it.

Jada bit her lip and sighed. The chances of her getting out of this class, rescuing Granny Jinks from the Crochet Club and getting her to the auditions seemed smaller and smaller.

CHAPTER SIX

'Here you go!' Miss Mendel said, arriving back at Jada's desk.

Jada pulled her eyes from the door and tried to smile as Miss Mendel put down a few more maths sheets on the table. But a small '*humph*' escaped her lips.

Miss Mendel's eyebrows drew together a little. 'Everything okay, Jada?' she asked.

'Err, yes,' Jada began, but she could tell Miss Mendel wasn't buying it. She decided to be honest. 'I just noticed that poster for the Magic Society auditions . . .'

Miss Mendel nodded, her eyes bright. 'Oh yes, I saw them setting that up in the big hall. Lots of magicians and exciting-looking characters were heading that way, I have to say.' The tutor smiled. 'I love a good trick! But maths has its own magic, too.'

'Maths is magic?' Femi asked. He pushed his glasses up his nose again. Even the Wang twins stopped whispering at that.

Miss Mendel fluttered her fingers in the air like she was sprinkling magic dust and Femi

67

sneezed as if the sparkles were really in the air. 'I like to think so!' Miss Mendel said with a laugh. 'Playing cards all have numbers on them, don't they? And they're used in a lot of tricks. And there are tricks to learning maths, too . . .'

As Miss Mendel began to explain some 'magic' short cuts to the maths problems they were working on, Femi sneezed again, and Jada remembered a conversation she'd had with Tilda earlier that day.

They'd just been messing about, really, but they'd joked that if Jada pretended to have a sneezing fit, and told her tutor that she had an allergy to dust, she could slip out of the class.

'After all, your lesson is in the library, right?' Tilda had said. 'All those old books are bound to make you sneeze!'

Jada suddenly remembered the silk handkerchief she'd stashed in the pocket of her shorts at Granny's house. She was wearing the same shorts today (they were her favourite pair) and sure enough the handkerchief was still there! She felt the smooth fabric and a few thoughts swam into her head. Maybe she could start blowing her nose in it and do some fake sneezing . . . ?

Nah, Jada thought, *this is Grandpa's hankie. It's special.* Plus, she definitely wasn't happy about lying, especially as Miss Mendel actually seemed really nice. *But how else can I get Granny Jinks to the auditions?*

Just then, Jada heard a muffled ringtone coming

from across the room. Miss Mendel rushed over to her sparkly handbag and pulled out her mobile.

'Sorry about this,' she said to the class, but Jada saw the tutor's face crumple into worry as she stared at her phone. 'Oh, gosh!' Miss Mendel exclaimed. Quickly, she swiped at the screen and held the phone to her ear. Jada knew it wasn't polite to listen in, but it was hard to avoid in the small room. 'Pipe burst . . . ?' Miss Mendel was saying, '. . . water going through the *floor* . . . ? Oh no! Er . . . Yes, I'll be there as soon as I can.'

She hung up the call and turned to the class, looking flustered. 'I'm ever so sorry, everyone, but I have an emergency at my flat. I'm going to have to take you next door to Mrs Whittaker's

Crochet Club for the last half of our session today. I'll get the librarian to help her out as well before calling your parents and carers so they know to collect you from there . . .' Poor Miss Mendel. She looked completely frazzled.

It took everything Jada had not to squeal with delight! She felt sorry for Miss Mendel and the mess she had to deal with at her home, but . . . *Result*. Now she could get Granny Jinks to the magic auditions. There might just be enough time to get there and show the society what her granny could do!

Jada and the other students gathered up their things, and Miss Mendel ushered them over to the Crochet Club and explained the situation to the crochet tutor before dashing out.

Mrs Whittaker gave the maths group some unravelled yarn to wind up into balls but Jada said she would sit with her granny. Mrs Whittaker nodded and Jada rushed over to Granny Jinks, who was muttering some angry and possibly rude words under her breath as she wrestled with some sparkly blue wool. Luna was snoozing in her cat bag, which was a good thing with all this yarn about.

'Granny!' Jada exclaimed, and Granny Jinks jumped, her glasses bouncing off the end of her

nose and into her lap, tangling with the wool.

'Jada Gem, you gave me a fright!' Granny Jinks said with a chuckle. 'Tutoring done already?'

Jada shrugged. 'Err, kind of . . . Our tutor got called away.' She raised an eyebrow, looking at the tangled lump of wool in Granny Jinks's hands. There were loose threads sticking out at random, and Jada wondered if it was *supposed* to look that lumpy. 'What are you making?' she asked.

Granny Jinks settled her glasses back on her nose and peered at the tangled mess. 'I have absolutely no idea . . . but I've started, so I'll finish!' she said in a determined voice.

'I was thinking . . .' Jada began, watching her

73

granny stabbing her hook a little *too* determinedly. 'There's quite a cool-looking class I saw a poster for – it's happening just down the hallway. Please could I go and take a look?'

'Hmm?' Granny Jinks said distractedly, her fingers flying as she wound the wool around her crochet hook haphazardly. She looked up quickly and nodded. 'Yes, yes, Jada, my dear, but then come straight back.'

Jada slipped out of the room, waving hello at Granny Jinks's favourite librarian, Maria, who had come to help Mrs Whittaker look after the maths kids. Then Jada was down the hallway, trying to figure out where the magic auditions were taking place. She spotted a tall, skinny man in a top hat and tails disappear into a room to the right.

A-ha! Jada thought. She rushed after him, and pushed the door open a crack. Peering inside, Jada saw people milling around, waving wands, shuffling cards and stroking white rabbits that poked out of hats. *This is it!* Jada thought, her excitement building. *The auditions!*

Jada grinned as she spotted Tilda sitting a little way from the door, tongue clamped between her teeth in concentration as she practised a card trick. *There's only one way to find out if I can get Granny Jinks on the list to audition*, Jada thought. *I've got to ask*. Granny always said, 'If you don't ask, you won't get and if you don't try you'll never know.' Taking a deep breath, Jada stepped inside.

CHAPTER SEVEN

Slipping inside the room, Jada immediately realised she didn't have to worry about anyone asking what she was doing there. Everyone was far too distracted. There was a real, thrilling sense of magic in the air. A young woman in a shiny blue-and-silver sari was energetically juggling some matching sparkly balls, impressively weaving around Jada as she edged further inside the room. A man with a fuzzy halo of grey hair was speaking softly to a pair of cooing white doves nestled together in a golden cage.

And, of course, there was Tilda. She was expertly shuffling her cards, the pack flying between her hands like it was defying gravity. Jada scooted over to her friend, calling her name. Tilda looked up at the sound of Jada's voice.

'Hey! You made it!' Tilda said excitedly. She began glancing around Jada, and her brow

knitted a little. 'Where's your gran, though?'

'She's stuck at the Crochet Club,' Jada said, still taking in all the activity in the room. She turned back to Tilda. 'Do you think there's time to get Granny Jinks back here to audition?'

Tilda nodded enthusiastically, her long hair bouncing. 'Of course! They haven't even properly started yet,' she said, still zipping her cards between her small hands.

Jada nodded determinedly. 'Amazing! Okay, so how do I sign Granny Jinks up?'

Just as she spoke, though, she heard someone behind her give a loud scoffing laugh.

Jada turned around, and saw a small, smug-looking boy with silky dark hair cut in a straight fringe across his forehead.

'You can't just turn up here today and get an audition for the *Dalton Green Magic Society*, you know!' he said.

He was dressed in black and grey, except for his white magician's gloves. As Jada looked at him, he flung his shiny cape over one shoulder. It was lined on the inside with red satin, and he seemed very pleased with it!

'Mind your own business, Henry,' Tilda said, rolling her eyes at Jada.

Henry put his hands on his hips. 'The Magic Society *is* my business,' the boy said snootily. 'My family have been a part of it for years and years. My *dad*'s a magician, my *grandad*'s a magician—'

'It just so happens, *my grandma* has everything it takes to become a fantastic magician, too,' Jada told Henry. She felt even more confident as Tilda stood next to her, nodding. 'It runs in my family as well, I'll have you know,' Jada added, narrowing her eyes.

Henry shrugged. 'Well, it's too late. Yesterday was the final day to sign up for the auditions, and all the slots are taken!' He pointed to a big sheet on the wall nearby. He lowered his finger when he actually looked properly at the sign-up list.

'A-ha,' Tilda exclaimed, also looking in the direction of Henry's white-gloved finger. There was a big, glaring space for one last audition spot on the sheet!

Jada grabbed a marker pen from a chair nearby, and rushed over to the wall. Drawing in a breath, she wrote in big bold letters in the final slot on the page:

THE MARVELLOUS GRANNY JINKS!

'There!' she said, resisting the urge to stick her tongue out triumphantly.

Henry frowned, looking back at Jada and Tilda. '*Granny Jinks . . . ?*' he murmured in surprise. He quickly shook his head. 'Whatever. All I know is these are the last auditions for the Magic Society for a whole year. Your granny better get here soon or her chances –' he pulled out a big silver coin, flipped it around near Jada's ear, then wiggled a gloved hand – 'will disappear!' he finished with a flourish. The coin was nowhere to be seen, and with a haughty grin, Henry spun away, his cape billowing behind him.

Jada and Tilda collapsed into giggles at his dramatic exit, but Jada knew that he was actually right. Now that she had signed Granny Jinks up

for the auditions, she had to get her over here to

perform!

'Right, I'm off to grab Granny,' she told Tilda.

Her friend nodded, hopping from foot to foot in nervous excitement. 'Yes, yes, go and get her! It'll be a Granny Grab. But be quick – the auditions are starting again soon!'

As Jada raced back down the hallway, she hoped that Granny Jinks really *did* have something she could perform for the judges. She'd have to pull something amazing out of the bag, given all the talent Jada had seen on display. . . *Maybe I should have told her about the auditions before?* Jada shook her head. There was no point worrying about that now.

In the crochet room, Femi and the Wang

twins were both being collected by their parents and waved goodbye to Jada in a friendly way. *Maybe maths tutoring really isn't all* that *bad*, Jada thought. But as she edged between the older men and women winding up their yarn and putting it away, Jada found her gran looking very unlike herself. Her mouth drooped at the corners, and she huffed as she looked at the pile of wool in her lap.

'Hey, Granny,' Jada said.

'Ah, Jada Gem, there you are,' Granny Jinks said. 'Ready to go? I know I am . . .'

Jada frowned, momentarily forgetting her mission to tell her grandmother all about the magic auditions. 'What's the matter, Granny?' she asked.

Granny Jinks gestured to the crochet project in her lap, a sigh fluttering out between her lips. 'Well, just look at this mess, my dear,' she said, shaking her head. 'I'm no good at crocheting, and all it's done is made me feel really old and useless. This stuff is supposed to come easily to a granny like me!'

Jada shook her head vigorously. 'No, Granny – it's because you're meant to be doing something far more exciting!' she said.

Granny Jinks smiled a tiny bit. 'That so? Go on, I'm listening.'

'So there are these auditions for the *Dalton Green Magic Society* happening *right now*, just next door.'

Granny nodded, looking just a little wistful. 'I saw the poster.'

'Well . . .' Jada paused dramatically. 'I signed you up!'

Granny Jinks was silent for a moment, and then her eyebrows shot up. 'You . . . you signed me up?' she exclaimed.

Luna stirred a little from where she'd been snoozing inside the cat bag.

Jada nodded, though she now felt a little less confident than before.

Granny gripped the arm of the worn armchair she had been sitting in, hoisted herself up to stand

and put her things on the chair. 'Ah, Jada Gem, that's very sweet, but this old bird is just going to get you home. If I can't master crochet, how am I going to pull off a magic act?'

Granny gave a not-funny chuckle, and Jada felt her own mouth turn down. This was not the Granny Jinks she knew. Her grandmother could do *anything* she put her mind to. Jada lifted her chin. *So I just need to find a way to convince Granny Jinks of that,* she thought.

CHAPTER EIGHT

'Granny, are you sure you don't want to just go and take a look at the other magicians' acts?' Jada asked, looking at her hopefully. 'You might feel differently once you've seen their performances . . .' she trailed off as Granny Jinks shook her head.

'I'm sorry, Jada Gem. I don't even have a trick prepared,' Granny Jinks insisted. 'I'd look a fool.'

'No way! You'd be amazing, I know it.' Jada thought hard. What could she say to persuade Granny to audition? 'I'm sure if Grandpa Jinks was here, he would say you should do it!' she tried again.

'Jada, my dear, your grandpa would never go to an audition without having practised.' Granny smiled fondly. 'He was a professional. He was the best of the bunch! And can you imagine how your dad would react if I told him I was going to try being a magician, too?' Granny laughed. 'No, no, no, dearest. There's a reason I was behind the scenes all those years . . .'

Jada pouted, but Granny Jinks seemed to have made up her mind.

'Come on, let's get you home,' Granny said, putting on her coat. But as she went to pick up her bags, Luna yelped and sprang out of her cat bag!

'Luna, come back!' Granny cried, rushing to catch her.

But the little black cat was too fast. There were squeals from all around the crochet room as Luna scampered over the tables, getting all tangled up in wool and glittery sequin craft supplies. Granny and Jada chased after her, but in a flash, Luna

had slipped out of the room and ran down the hallway, miaow-barking the whole way.

Granny and Jada followed and finally caught up with Luna, who was waiting patiently in front of a door.

Jada's eyes widened as she realised where they were. Right outside the room where the Magic Society auditions were taking place!

'Granny, look. This is where the auditions are happening!' She grinned at her grandmother.

Granny Jinks looked surprised, raising her eyebrows. 'You just don't give up, do you Jada Gem?' she said, chuckling.

Luna growl-purred happily as she was put back into her cat bag, her little head poking out.

Jada laughed too, and gave
Luna's ears a scratch. 'Even
Luna thinks you should try out
for the Magic Society!' Jada said.

'She looks just like a magician's cat now!'

The little feline let out another miaow–bark in
agreement.

Jada watched as Granny Jinks began to pick
sequins off the cat's dark furry head thoughtfully.
The look on her face made Jada think that her
grandmother might *just* be coming around.

'She does *look* pretty magical with all this
glitter in her coat . . .' Granny Jinks said slowly.
'And of all the places she could have run to, she
brought me here.'

Jada could see the old sparkle beginning to return to her grandmother's eyes, and she felt a surge of hope. '*Pleeeeaase* give the magic auditions a try, Granny,' she said in her sweetest, most appealing voice. 'I'll . . . I'll do the dishes every single time I come round for a whole month! I'll water every single plant in the house! Oh, how about I let you have all my fried plantain every time you cook for a month, too? Or . . . hmm, actually – maybe just a week.'

Granny Jinks let out one of her real laughs, big and bubbly. Jada grinned.

'Just a week, eh?' her grandmother said through her chuckles. 'Fair enough! But, Jada Gem, I really haven't practised in years. It's a lot of pressure.'

Jada's eyes widened at this. 'But, Granny Jinks, what do you always tell me? Diamonds are formed . . .'

'. . . under pressure,' Granny Jinks finished with a smile. She looked thoughtful. 'Your grandfather used to say that to *me*, you know.' She turned back to Jada and gave her the **Jinks wink**, just like the one her grandpa was doing in the poster Granny Jinks had on the wall at home. 'You know what? There was one card trick that I was always fabulous at — but I don't have my special pack with me.'

Jada jumped up and down excitedly. 'Yessssss!' she exclaimed. 'You can definitely do it, Granny!

And I know just the person who can help with the cards!'

Jada grabbed Granny Jinks's hand, opened the door to the room, and pulled her inside. 'Quick, this way, Granny!' Jada said. She hoped they were still in time for Granny's audition slot.

The *Dalton Green Magic Society* auditions were in full swing! Jada pulled along Granny Jinks, and with Luna bouncing on her grandmother's hip in her special cat bag, they made their way further into the big room where the auditions were taking place.

Right there on the stage at the front, with a spotlight trained on her, was Tilda!

'Is this your card?' she was asking one of the

judges in a loud, confident voice, fanning out a pack and allowing one to float a little above the others. The red-headed lady shook her head. Jada felt a twinge of worry in her stomach as she watched.

'Hmm . . .' Tilda said. Right then, she glanced up and saw Jada and her grandmother. She grinned widely, and then turned back to the

judges. 'Could you just take a quick look under your glass, then?' Tilda asked the red-headed judge. The woman lifted her glass . . . and let out a happy exclamation.

'Oh! Here's my card! The jack of spades. Wonderful!'

The whole room burst into applause, whispering to each other. How had Tilda done the trick? She bowed dramatically and announced, 'Thank you so much! I've been Tilda the Terrific!'

There was a short moment while the judges whispered to one another at their table in front of the stage. Then a man with shiny dark hair cleared his throat.

'Tilda the Terrific — welcome to the *Dalton Green Magic Society*!' he announced.

Tilda bowed again, with a big, delighted smile on her face. Jada and Granny Jinks clapped and whooped, but then the room quietened down as the dark-haired man spoke again.

'Right,' he said, 'I think that's all of the auditions for today—'

'Wait!' Tilda said from the stage. 'There's one more person here to audition!'

She waved her hands at Jada, beckoning her to bring Granny Jinks forward.

Jada yanked on her grandmother's hand and pulled her towards the front of the room. She noticed that Granny Jinks's palm was clammy.

Granny must be nervous, she thought to herself. It made Jada feel shy, too, but she kept on walking towards the front of the room.

Meanwhile, Tilda was confidently speaking to the judges.

'My friend's gran is here to do some amazing magic for all of you . . .' Tilda was saying.

'It's going to be great, Granny,' Jada whispered, but Granny Jinks still stood nervously at the side of the stage.

'I'm not so sure about this, Jada Gem,' Gran hissed. 'I don't think I can go up there.'

'Sometimes we have to do stuff that scares us,' Jada said, kindly. 'My granny is always saying stuff like that.'

Granny Jinks looked both scared and amused at the same time, but she still didn't move.

Jada knew what she had to do. She squeezed her grandmother's hand, took a very deep breath and then let the hand go. Before she could think too much about what she was doing, she made her way up the short set of steps leading to the stage, and went to stand beside Tilda. She whispered, 'Can we borrow your cards?' Her friend nodded and handed them over, then linked pinky-fingers with Jada to say 'good luck'.

If Jada had thought she was nervous about speaking in front of her maths class, it was nothing compared to seeing the dark silhouettes of the judges in front of her! But if she could do it, then Granny Jinks might be inspired enough to come and do some magic for them, too!

'Yes, that's right,' Jada began. 'You're about to witness some tricks, the likes of which you've never seen!' she said, her voice getting stronger and louder with each word. 'You won't believe your eyes. She could well be the most amazing magician ever!' She was shouting now, with

every person in the room hanging onto her every word. 'Ladies and gentlemen, put your hands together for the wonderful, the fabulous . . .

THE MARVELLOUS GRANNY JINKS!'

CHAPTER NINE

Jada clapped very loudly. Tilda was clapping as well, and soon everyone else joined in. She saw Granny take a gulping breath and then, to Jada's relief, her grandmother slowly walked up onto the stage. Granny Jinks smiled at the judges and took the cards from Jada, handing her Luna, who was squirming in her cat bag.

The girls moved off to the side of the stage,

and Granny Jinks shielded her eyes against the bright spotlight.

'That's right! I'm probably the most advanced magician you've ever met!' Granny's voice was a little shaky at first, but she was soon chuckling. 'Advanced in age, that is, but there are some new tricks in this old girl yet . . .' She glanced over at Jada, who nodded encouragingly. Granny Jinks opened the special pack of slippery playing cards and began to shuffle them.

But, just as she did so, a voice came out of the darkness from the judging table.

'I'm afraid we cannot assess any more card tricks in this audition.' It was the dark-haired man who'd spoken before. 'We've seen too many tonight. I doubt you'll top little Tanya's performance, anyway. Do you have anything else?'

'It's Tilda, not Tanya!' Jada's friend protested from the side of the stage.

Tilda was fizzing with annoyance, but Jada was more worried about her grandmother. She could see that Granny Jinks's shoulders had drooped.

'Err, I don't really have anything else . . .' Granny Jinks looked around helplessly.

Luna let out a miaow-bark, like she was trying to think of ways to encourage her!

Jada bit her lip. She'd sent her grandmother up in front of an audience completely unprepared. *What would Grandpa Jinks say?* Jada gasped under her breath. *Grandpa Jinks!* She felt about in her pocket and – yes! It was still there! Her fingers curled round the fake thumb from Grandpa Jinks's box. Also inside Jada's pocket was the silky, spotted hankie that she had considered using for her sneezing idea to get out of tutoring. If she could somehow sneak the fake thumb over to Granny Jinks in the hankie, then maybe her grandmother could use it to do a trick for the judges?

Granny Jinks was still standing awkwardly in the spotlight. Quickly, Jada rushed to her side.

'Just give us a magic minute, ladies and gentlemen!' Jada said loudly. She pulled the thumb wrapped in the hankie out of her pocket and nudged Granny Jinks, trying to nod subtly towards her hand.

'Here, Granny!' Jada murmured out of the corner of her mouth.

'Ah!' Granny Jinks whispered back, spotting the thumb and hankie. She cleared her throat and said, 'My granddaughter, Jada here, is quite right. I have another little trick up my sleeve! Just give me a moment . . .'

Jada frowned in confusion, but then Granny

Jinks whispered, 'Drop it on the count of three.'

A moment later, Granny Jinks made a big, wide flourish with her hands, while quickly whispering, **'ONE ... TWO ... THREE!'** to Jada. Jada dropped the handkerchief and thumb just as Granny Jinks made a big show of dropping her glasses and handbag on the floor!

'Oh my goodness,' Granny said theatrically. 'I'm all fingers and thumbs. I do apologise . . .'

Granny Jinks began gathering up the things on the floor, and Jada noticed that she had tucked the handkerchief into her sleeve. But the thumb — where was it?

Suddenly, Jada spotted the prop in the darkness. It had rolled a metre away. *Oh no . . .* Before Jada could do anything, Luna leaped out of her cat bag again and batted the thumb – which skidded right towards Granny Jinks! In one smooth movement, Jada saw her gran sweep up the fake thumb and slip it over her real one.

Phew! Jada thought.

'Goodness me, the cat's out of the bag now,' Granny Jinks joked, straightening up again. The judges all laughed, and Jada could see her gran's shoulders sink in relief. Granny Jinks added, 'Jada Gem, my lovely assistant, can you fetch our feline friend?'

Jada rushed forward with a 'nothing-to-see-here' grin and quickly grabbed Luna. Her heart was pounding. Was Granny really going to pull off the trick? But something had happened to her. She shone like a star under the spotlight, and walked confidently towards the edge of the stage with a spring in her step.

'Excuse me, dear, it's thirsty work up here, no

word of a lie. Do you mind if I . . . ?' Granny Jinks leaned down and reached for one of the judge's cans of fizzy drink. After opening it, taking a big gulp and burping loudly to more laughs from the judges and the crowd, Granny Jinks made a big show of putting the can down. But, try as she might, it seemed to float up in her hand.

Wow! Jada knew it must be the suction pad in the fake thumb that was helping with the trick, but Granny Jinks made it look like real magic! The whole room burst into applause as Granny Jinks finally managed to 'put down' the can.

Then, Granny whipped the hankie out from where she had tucked it into her sleeve. She made a big show of mopping her brow with it, then flapped the handkerchief in front of her. Everyone gasped – including Jada – because now the hankie was GONE. *How did she do that?* Jada looked at Tilda for an explanation, but her friend was equally astonished.

Then Granny waved her hands and the handkerchief appeared once more.

As Granny grinned widely, the whole room seemed to lean closer towards her. Then they burst into even louder applause! The hankie now had a word on it, seemingly burned into the silk with smoke:

'Woah!' Jada exclaimed, and she heard Tilda whooping and clapping too. *That was amazing.*

Except . . . the hankie seemed to be smouldering!

'Oh, er . . .' Granny Jinks muttered, seeming a bit less confident now. She dropped the handkerchief on the stage and backed away as white smoke kept puffing from the fabric. The dark-haired judge strode onto the stage and stomped on the hankie firmly until it stopped smouldering.

'That's quite enough of that!' he said, shooting Granny an accusatory stare.

Granny Jinks gathered Jada, Tilda and Luna towards the side of the stage. 'Oh dear,' she said. 'That got a bit out of hand. Or should I say, thumb?'

Jada giggled. 'How did you do that, Granny?' she whispered.

Granny Jinks gave her a wink. 'That's one of your grandpa's magic handkerchiefs. He'd use the lighter in the tip of that prop thumb to do that very trick. But I told you I was rusty!' she added with a chuckle.

'That was *amazing*, Granny Jinks,' Tilda said, looking up at Jada's grandmother in awe.

Jada agreed. She was bursting with pride — but she was also worried. After all, the head judge had stomped on the handkerchief. Would they let Granny Jinks join the *Dalton Green Magic Society*?

CHAPTER TEN

Jada tapped her foot nervously as she waited for the judges to make their decision. They were all gathered round the judging table with their heads close together, whispering. Jada, her gran and Tilda made their way off the stage, with Luna safely back in her bag.

'Hmm, that wasn't all bad, I suppose,' said a voice from nearby. Jada saw Henry, the boy she'd spoken to earlier, sidling over to where they were standing. He was still wearing his fancy cape and gloves. 'Although,' he continued with a snicker, 'the ending was!'

Jada rolled her eyes. 'Shame I missed *your* trick,' she said, though she clearly didn't mean it.

'Yeah, it is!' Henry said, ignoring her tone. 'And I suppose you were right about *some* magic running in your family. I've heard my grandpa mention the name Jinks once or twice.' Henry nodded over to the judging table. 'He's the *head judge* of the Magic Society, you know. Of course, you do. Everyone knows *Zhao the Magnificent*!'

What? Jada felt her heart sink again. Henry's grandfather was one of the judges?

119

'Did that young man just say *Zhao the Magnificent*?' Granny Jinks asked Jada, as Henry swished his cape and strode away.

'Yes,' Jada replied.

Granny Jinks patted her head and pulled her glasses out of her afro, perching them on her nose to look over at the judges' table. 'My goodness, of course. That's him! Your grandpa's old rival. Oh, dear, that could mean a bit of trouble for us, Jada Gem . . .' Granny said, looking worried. She turned back to look at her granddaughter, and her face brightened a bit. 'Not to worry, my sweet. Either way, I had plenty, *plenty* fun tonight!'

Jada gripped Granny Jinks's hand tightly

as Henry's grandfather rang a little bell and everyone in the room quietened down.

'We have reached a decision,' he began in a loud voice. Jada's pulse was going a mile a minute. 'Although we definitely did not all agree,' he added, looking annoyed.

The red-headed judge stood up beside him and rolled her eyes. She was smiling. 'That's right, the judges have made our decision and . . .' She paused, and Jada thought her heart might beat out of her chest! '. . . *the Marvellous Granny Jinks* is the final member to join the *Dalton Green Magic Society*. Congratulations!'

Jada squealed and Granny Jinks laughed her booming laugh, jumping up and down just as her

granddaughter was doing. 'I got in? I got in!' she cried.

'Yes,' the judge continued. 'We loved the drama of the performance, and the show-womanship was fabulous. We were never quite sure what was real and what was an act. And a lot of that was down to your wonderful helper, too,' she said, nodding at Jada. 'So . . . we'd like to invite her to join the society as well – as your assistant!'

Jada and Granny Jinks jumped up and down again! Jada felt on top of the world as her granny scooped her up into her arms for a HUGE hug, spinning her round and round until she was dizzy.

'Oh my goodness, Jada, my diamond gem!' Granny Jinks exclaimed. 'This here? This is *real* magic!'

Tilda rushed over, cheering, too. 'This is amazing, Jada. We'll get to be in the Magic Society together! We'll do performances, and skills practice, and hear talks from visiting magicians . . .' She listed all the activities in a breathless rush. 'And, best of all, it's secret!'

Jada was absolutely fit to burst with excitement and pride. This was the best day ever! Granny Jinks was going to be able to follow her dream of being a magician, and it was all thanks to her!

'Oh, Jada. Your grandpa would have been so proud of you,' Granny Jinks said happily.

Jada grinned. 'He'd be even more proud of *you*, Granny! You were amazing.' Then suddenly, Tilda's final words hit Jada. 'Uh-oh, wait! This *is* a secret society. Can we tell Dad about it?' she said to her grandmother. 'You know how he feels about magic.'

Granny Jinks frowned. 'We should definitely tell him, but maybe not *right* away. Not until we've had a chance to learn a few more tricks.' She looked at her watch. '*And* . . . he's going to be picking you up from my house really soon!'

Jada and her grandmother quickly said goodbye to Tilda, who was waiting for her sister, and Granny Jinks got lots more congratulations from her fellow magicians as they made their way outside.

They raced back to Granny Jinks's house. Quickly, they shed their coats and settled into the living room just as they heard Jada's dad's car door shut outside.

'Mum? Jada?' Jonny Jinks called, striding into the room. 'Ah, here you are,' he said with a smile.

Jada glanced over at her granny, who was holding a book upside down, pretending to read it. She coughed, and Granny Jinks turned it around quickly.

'Hello, Jonny, dear. Good day?'

Jada's dad came over and gave her a hug. 'Not bad,' he began, answering Granny Jinks's question, and then he frowned. 'But I heard what happened today . . .'

Jada's wide eyes met her gran's as they stared at one another. Uh-oh!

'Er . . . you did?' Granny coughed nervously.

'Of course! Miss Mendel had to leave your maths tutoring early, right?'

Jada exhaled her biggest ever sigh. 'Oh, er, yes she did!' she replied. Out of the corner of her eye, she saw Granny Jinks fan herself with the book. She stopped quickly as Jada's dad turned towards her.

'The tutor asked if the lesson could be a little bit later next week, and that might mean you'll need to skip Crochet Club, Mum. Is that okay?' he asked Granny Jinks.

Granny Jinks grinned widely. 'Oh, I'm sure

I can conjure up something else to fill the time,' she said, giving Jada a secret, big, fat **Jinks wink**.

Jada winked back and Luna let out a loud miaow-bark.

Magic!

NOW IT'S YOUR TURN TO TRY SOME MAGIC TRICKS OF YOUR OWN!

TILDA'S CARD TRICK

Would you like to learn how to do Tilda's card-under-the-glass trick from her audition? For this trick you'll need:

- A pack of playing cards, extra slippery like Tilda's so you can move them fast!
- A glass.
- An eager audience member.

This trick is all about being fast and a bit sneaky.

First of all, ask a member of your audience to pick a card – any card. Fan out the cards in front of you in one hand, so they can see the faces and when they pick one, raise the card up higher than the rest of the deck. Ask them to remember the card they chose, and while they're concentrating on that, slip the card into your other hand – keep them talking and distracted while you slip it under their glass. This might take some practice, especially keeping your audience focused on you throughout the trick so they don't notice their card!

THE DISAPPEARING HANDKERCHIEF

The trick that Granny Jinks performs in her audition for the *Dalton Green Magic Society* is also another great trick that uses the fake thumb tip! You can get them at most magic shops in different sizes and colours. For this trick, you'll need:

- A magician's 'thumb tip'.
- A small handkerchief or cloth.

This trick is a bit different as you have to be both slow and fast. First, show your audience the handkerchief by holding it out between both hands, making sure you cover the fake thumb tip with the handkerchief. As you fold the handkerchief up between your hands, slip the fake thumb tip off and stuff the handkerchief inside it, hiding the thumb tip in your closed fist. This is the part where you need to be very quick, and also sure that your handkerchief isn't too big! You then slip the thumb tip back on with the handkerchief inside! This is a great trick once you've found the right tools and are comfortable with using both the thumb and the handkerchief.

GRANNY JINKS'S FLOATING CAN TRICK

For this trick, you'll need:

- A magician's 'thumb tip' with a special suction pad on the tip.
- An ordinary drinks can.

This simple trick might take a few tries to get right as you get used to using the fake thumb. When you pick the can up to take a drink, gently press the tip of the thumb with the suction pad against the can – this will keep it 'floating' as you release your hand. Give it a few tries to get the pressure right on the can before you demonstrate it to an audience – you don't want to spill your drink all over them!

**LOOK OUT FOR MORE MAGIC
FROM GRANNY JINKS AND JADA!
COMING SOON IN . . .**

THE
MARVELLOUS
GRANNY
JINKS
AND ME

Animal Magic!